Shelter of Daylight
January 2025

Short Stories

Flash Fiction

Poetry

*

THE STAFF OF SHELTER OF DAYLIGHT:

MANAGING EDITOR: Tyree Campbell
WEBMASTER: H David Blalock

Cover art "Misty Morning" by Vonnie Winslow Crist
Cover design by Laura Givens

Vol. VI, No. 1   January 2025
Shelter of Daylight is published twice a year, on the 1st days of January and July in the United States of America by Hiraeth Publishing, P.O. Box 1248, Tularosa, NM 88352. Copyright 2025 by Hiraeth Publishing. All rights revert to authors and artists upon publication except as noted in selected individual contracts. Nothing may be reproduced in whole or in part without written permission from the authors and artists. Any similarity between places and persons mentioned in the fiction or semi-fiction and real places or persons living or dead is coincidental. Writers and artists guidelines are available online at www.hiraethsffh.com. Guidelines are also available upon request from Hiraeth Publishing, P.O. Box 1248, Tularosa, NM 88352, if request is accompanied by a self-addressed #10 envelope with a first-class US stamp. Editor: Tyree Campbell.

A Little Help, Please

In the world of the small indie press we fight a never-ending battle for attention to our work, as writers and in publishing. Here's an example: big publishers [you know who they are] have gobs of $$$ that they can devote to advertising and marketing. Here at Hiraeth Publishing, our advertising budget consists of the deposits for whatever soda bottles and aluminum cans we can find alongside the highways. Anti-littering laws make our task even more difficult . . . ☺

That's where YOU come in. YOU are our best promoter. YOU are the one who can tell others about us. Just send 'em to our website, tell them about our store. That's all. Just that.

Of course, we don't mind if you talk us up. We're pretty good, you know. We have some award-winning and award-nominated writers and artists, plus other voices well-deserving to be heard [not everyone wins awards, right?] but our publications are read-worthy nevertheless.

That number once again is:

www.hiraethsffh.com

Friend us on Facebook at Hiraeth Publish

Follow us on Twitter at

@ HiraethPublish1

As the societies of Earth collapse into chaos and destruction, Bailey Belvedere, a U.S. Army Intelligence officer fighting for her very survival, steals aboard an alien spacecraft, and soon finds herself given the authority and power by a superior alien entity to intervene in various problems in the Galaxy. Along the way she frees a world from interstellar slave traffickers, deals with an AI who becomes pregnant, inadvertently destroys a waffle house, fights against the abductors of a special child, and generally finds herself in some sort of trouble from one moment to the next.

Type: Novel – science fiction

Ordering Link:
Print Edition:
https://www.hiraethsffh.com/product-page/further-adventures-of-bailey-belvedere-by-tyree-campbell

PDF Edition: https://www.hiraethsffh.com/product-page/further-adventures-of-bailey-belvedere-by-tyree-campbell-1

The Wolf Who Cried

Maureen Bowden

A full moon coincided with Angelina's birth, on the night before the feast of Samhain, in the year 2001. The hour was heavy with ancient magic. Of course she was a werewolf. How could she not be? Her mother was a witch; her father was who knows what? Mother never told and Angelina never asked.

Their home was a cottage in the foothills of Wales' Cambrian Mountains, on the outskirts of Brechfa Forest. The day before her seventh birthday her mother said, "Lina, you're old enough to attend the coven now. We'll be meeting at moonrise to celebrate the coming of Samhain and honour the souls of the dead."

That didn't sound much like fun but Angelina must be respectful of the witches. They'd always been kind to her even though she thought some of them were mad as a kettle-full of kippers. She asked, "What will I have to do?"

"Nothing. Just watch. You won't be initiated until you reach your second seventh year, and then only if it's what you want. Nobody will force you into witchcraft."

Reasonable enough. "I think I'd rather be a football player and be paid a stash of cash."

Mother smiled. "Your choice, Lina, but whatever you do with your life you must promise never to tell anyone about the witches. The Finders mustn't hear of us."

She'd overheard Mother and Grandmother whispering about the Finders. The little she'd heard frightened her. "Who are they and what will happen if they find you?"

Mother sat beside her on the couch, in front of the log fire, safe in their cosy cottage, and she told her, "They're descendants of Matthew Hopkins, the seventeenth century Witch Finder General. There are four of them. We call the leader the Vile One. The others are his father the Old One, and the Vile One's two sons, Demetrius and Chiron. That's not their real names but we've given them the names of the evil brothers in Shakespeare's shock-horror, 'Titus Andronicus.' The Bard was having a bad day when he wrote that one."

Angelina shivered. She hadn't read 'Titus Andronicus' but she knew what happened to witches in the seventeenth century. They were hanged, drowned or burned. The burning must have been the worst. "How can they go around killing witches now, Mother? It's against the law."

Mother sighed. "So are a lot of things, Lina, but they're rich and powerful, and such people can flout the law. They hide in plain sight and keep their ears flapping for any rumour of a witch. Always be on your guard."

Samhain drew near and the witches gathered in a woodland clearing dominated by an oak tree that had stood for more than a thousand years. Angelina watched as they encircled the tree, their voices rising in song to the goddess Hekate as they danced. Grandmother, the eldest witch, led the dance. When the moon rose, Angelina felt the beast stir in her consciousness and she was filled with the urge to shake off her human form.

In the depths of the forest a lone grey wolf sensed the little girl's awakening and he howled a prayer to Selene, goddess of the moon, to keep her safe.

The following day Angelina described her experience to Mother. "It was a wonderful feeling, wild and exciting, but I don't understand it."

"We were all aware of the stirring of the beast and we rejoiced for you." She laughed, "You weren't meant to be a footballer, Lina. The Beautiful Game will have to manage without you. You won't be a witch, either."

"So, what will I be?"

"What you are now. The goddesses Hekate and Selene have blessed you with a dual identity. You're a werewolf, but your metamorphosis won't happen until you reach your second seven. You have plenty of time to get used to the idea."

Angelina felt that football would have been more lucrative but the prospect of being a wolf fascinated and exhilarated her.

* * *

On the night of the full moon following her fourteenth birthday she felt her body start to change. She stepped outside the cottage, into the moonlight. Her bones stretched and reshaped. Her face and limbs elongated, and soft fur covered her flesh. The forest called to her and she sprang towards it. Bounding into its depths, she revelled in sounds and smells of the wild, beyond human sensibility, and colours outside the spectrum, visible only to animal eyes. The spirit of the ancient woodland engulfed her, claiming her as its own.

She caught the scent of another wolf, a male, close by but remaining hidden. She searched but he eluded her. His presence was unsettling but not threatening.

In the months that followed, each time the full moon rose and she morphed into the wolf, she was aware of the male, watching but keeping his distance. She called him her shadow wolf.

One night her life changed. She fell asleep in the forest after morphing back to human form and in a dream she heard the shadow's mind voice, "Be brave, Angelina and be strong."

When she awoke, the dream left her feeling uneasy. Why did she need to be brave and strong? Was the shadow sending her a warning? She ran home, her instinct screaming that something was wrong. Grandmother was waiting at the cottage door. Where was Mother? Trying to stem her panic, she said, "Where is she? What's happened?"

The old lady took her in her arms. "I'm sorry, Lina. The Finders took her."

Angelina pushed her away and shook her head. "No, no. They didn't burn her. Please tell me they didn't burn her."

"They did, but ease your heart, child. She didn't suffer. Hekate takes her daughters' souls before the flames

8

touch their flesh. Your mother is at peace with the Goddess."

Angelina's rage overcame her need to weep. "I'll kill them all. I'll track them down one by one and I'll kill them, slowly."

"Yes, Lina," Grandmother said. "I believe you will."

* * *

Grandmother moved into Angelina's cottage. It was the next best thing to having her mother and she grew to love and respect the elderly witch.

She trained herself to control the wolf during the time of the full moon so she could morph only when it was convenient. The wolf must be disciplined when she hunted the Finders. For five years she studied their lifestyle: where they lived; where and with whom they socialised; their vices and weaknesses; every aspect of their lives. Facebook, Twitter and the vast murky depths of social media had their uses.

When she was nineteen years old she took driving lessons and passed her test at the first attempt. She would need mobility in her human form in order to reach the Finders. She told Grandmother, "I'm ready for them. I'll take the old one first. He's bedridden now and I don't want him to die a peaceful, geriatric death." Her smile was feral. "I know where and how he lives and I know how to be alone with him when the full moon rises. The wolf will bite but not deep enough to kill. He'll bleed to death, drop by painful drop."

Grandmother frowned. "Take care, Lina. You're in danger of losing your humanity and becoming only wolf."

"Would that be such a bad thing? Mother told me I could make my own choices."

"Of course you can, but be sure you make the right choice."

"I'll think about that once I've killed the Finders."

After outlining to Grandmother her plan to dispose of the Old One, she said, "The police will be questioning possible witnesses. Can you put a glamour on me to change my appearance?"

Grandmother chuckled. "Who do think I am? Morgan le Fay? Wait a minute." She trotted into her bedroom and returned carrying a long auburn wig. "If you don't draw attention to yourself it will be difficult for anyone to remember your face. Wear this and they'll only remember the hair."

In the month of January, in the afternoon before the rising of the full moon, Angelina drove Grandmother's second hand, grey Corsa to southeast England. The trusty vehicle was not a car to catch anyone's attention. She'd studied the Google map and memorised the route to the Old One's stately home. The moon was rising when she parked in a quiet country road about a quarter of a mile from her destination. She walked the rest of the way, keeping the wolf at bay until she was ready to morph. When she reached the Old One's driveway she tucked her dark hair into Grandmother's wig, donned a pair of gloves to avoid leaving fingerprints, approached the large oak door and clanged the brass knocker that resembled a humanoid gargoyle.

A footman or some such flunky opened the door, bowed, and said "Good evening, Miss. Is His Lordship expecting you?"

She fluttered her eyelashes, heavy with mascara. "Yes. Willow Lupetta, physiotherapist."

He smirked, "Of course, Miss. Follow me." He led her up an ornate, winding staircase to a bedroom door.

She said, "Ensure that we're not disturbed. I'll let myself out."

He bowed and retreated, no doubt to share the salacious snippet with the domestic staff.

She entered the bedroom. The Old One, propped up on an explosion of pillows, squinted over his spectacles, threw down his copy of 'The Times' and said, "This is a pleasant surprise, my dear. Did the Escort Agency send you?"

"Your Fairy Godmother sent me." She sashayed across to the bedside light and switched it off. "We don't need that. The moon is more romantic." She drew back the curtains and moonlight flooded the room. She stripped off her clothes.

His Lordship leered at her. "What a bobby dazzler. Are you a witch?"

She flung off the auburn wig and said, "No, but my mother was." She freed the wolf.

Before the Old One had chance to scream she was upon him and sinking her fangs into his neck, but not deep enough to kill him. Blood spurted from the wound. He would be dead when a flunky brought his breakfast.

She morphed back to human form, dressed, not forgetting the gloves and the wig, and then she left.

She strolled back to the car, removed the wig and drove home.

The Vile One was next. She needed to ascertain his location at the time of the next full moon. 'Hello' magazine revealed that he would be attending a business conference with financiers and Stock Market speculators to discuss possible lucrative deals with Saudi Arabian oil magnates. The conference would be held at Pond Hall, the residence of a minor aristocrat, Earl Polmondbury, pronounced Pondy. It was situated in Norfolk, a few miles from where King John lost the crown jewels.

Angelina told Grandmother, "I intend to incapacitate the Vile One's chauffeur for a few hours and take his place. I'll need a sleeping potion that tastes good, a chauffeur's uniform and another wig. Can you help?"

The old lady chuckled. "No problem. Young Sophie, the witch with an eye for the lads, has a variety of wigs that save her a fortune in hairdresser charges. Old Margie will set up her sewing machine and run up a uniform." She winked. "And witchcraft will provide the sleeping potion. The ingredients are growing in the garden."

On the day of the conference, Angelina, wearing a black jacket with brass buttons, sensible knee-length black skirt, black stockings and blonde corkscrew curls topped with a jaunty black cap, drove Grandmother's Corsa to Norfolk. A black shoulder bag on the seat beside her contained her gloves, a few banknotes and a sachet of white powder.

A short distance from Pond Hall she located a lay-by that suited her purpose, parked the Corsa, donned her gloves, slung her bag across her shoulders and set off to find the Finder.

The hall's extensive ornamental gardens, dotted with duck-shaped topiary creations, incorporated a guest's parking area. She recognised the Vile One's Bugatti Divo from a photograph in 'Hello.'

The VIPs were getting acquainted in the Hall's ballroom that doubled as a conference suite. The chauffeurs, bodyguards and social companions were accommodated in a luxurious lounge containing a refreshment bar with appropriate staff. She joined them and mingled. Snatches of conversation identified the Vile One's chauffeur. She strolled across to his table and smiled. "May I join you?"

He smiled back. "Feel free. You a chauffeur?"

She sat down. "Yes. You too?"

"Yeah. Not much fun when you have to stay sober, is it?"

Thank the Goddess. She had her opening. "Ah, I think I can help there. The bar staff do a slightly alcoholic cocktail that tastes good but will keep you well below the limit. I'll fetch us a couple."

She sauntered to the bar. "Two glasses of sparkling water, please." She opened her bag, pulled out a ten-pound note and the witchy sachet. She passed the £10 to the bar attendant and while he was pocketing the generous tip she did another tipping, out of the sachet and into one of the glasses. Returning to the table she made sure she placed the potion in front of the Vile One's chauffeur and she took a sip of her own glass of water. "Oh, that's really good. Try it."

He raised his glass. "Cheers." He tried it. "Yeah, that is good. My name's Tim. What's yours?"

She plucked a name out of her memory of former school friends. "Georgia. Glad to meet you. Tim."

After a couple more sips of the potion Tim's eyes were glazing over and his voice was slurred. Before the glass was empty he was snoring. Angelina emptied the dregs into the potted plant behind the table, delved into Tim's pockets and stole the Divo's keys. She slipped them into her bag and approached the bar attendant that she'd enriched by £10.

"Excuse me," she said. "A gentleman over there appears to have had a little too much to drink. Is there somewhere he could sleep it off?"

"Off course, Miss. We'll take him to a Guest bedroom." He signalled to one of his colleagues and they carried Tim away.

Angelina left the lounge, made her way to the car park, unlocked the Divo, climbed into the driver's seat, made herself comfortable and waited.

The moon was riding high in the sky when the Vile One staggered drunkenly to the car, opened the door and slumped across the back seats.

"Ready to go home, Sir?" She asked.

He gave a puzzled grunt. "Where's my chauffeur?"

"He was taken ill. An ambulance has been called. I'm his substitute. Everything's under control. I know the route." She started the engine and drove away from the topiary ducks and out of the car park.

He grunted again. "What's your name, girlie?"

"Angelina." There was no danger in telling him. He'd be dead by morning.

"Pretty name. Are you angelic?"

"Depends how you define angelic."

He laughed. "I like you, girlie. I could show you how much but first there's something I need more than anything."

"What's that, Sir?"

"A pee."

Perfect. The Goddess was co-operating. "I anticipated you would. There's a quiet lay-by along this road. It backs onto a patch of wild ground, plenty of bushes and undergrowth. Will that suffice?"

"Certainly. Do you think of everything, girlie?"

"I try, Sir."

She pulled into the lay-by and switched off the engine. The Corsa sat in wait a few feet away. If the Vile

One saw it, he was too drunk to be concerned by its presence. She climbed out of the Divo and opened the passenger door for him. While he made his way unsteadily into the bushes she slipped out of her clothes.

After emptying his bladder he turned back towards the lay-by and was confronted by the wolf. With panic in his eyes he looked around for somewhere to run, but she leaped at him, all fur and fangs, and she bit. She dragged him into the undergrowth damp with his urine and left him, whimpering in fear and pain, bleeding to death. He'd be dead before anyone found him.

Returning to human form, she dressed, donned her gloves and slung her bag across her shoulders. After locking the car she hurled the keys into the bushes to lie beside the Vile One's body so that an opportunist thief couldn't steal the abandoned, prestigious vehicle and become a murder suspect.

She settled into Grandmother's Corsa and drove home. Two down, two to go.   Maybe she'd read Titus Andronicus to see what she was up against.

The Old One and the Vile One's deaths made the news, of course, but the reports were brief, giving no indication of how they died, citing only 'natural causes.' The Powers That Be had apparently chosen to avoid bizarre speculation. Social media's main interest in the matter was the fractious disputes over inheritance between prospective beneficiaries. There was no mention of grief or deep mourning. The deceased had few true friends and many enemies.

In the year 2021 a full moon would once again coincide with Angelina's birthday on the night before Samhain. It would be an auspicious time to kill the brothers.

After scrolling through social media for an update on their activities she didn't need the Bard's shock-horror to warn her of their personalities. They were arrogant, former public school spoilt brats and they were dangerous. She'd deal with them on her own territory, not on theirs. She asked Grandmother to call the coven together so she could speak to them.

After she told the witches her intentions Grandmother said, "No, Lina. Surely you're not bringing the Finders here. You'll endanger us all."

"Yes, I am, but you won't be in danger. On the night of the dead and the full moon we'll be protected by both Hekate and Selene. Delay your Samhain celebrations and stay out of the forest until I've killed the brothers. You can burn their bodies as a sacrifice to Hekate. Deal?"

The witches whispered and mumbled to each other. She knew they weren't happy but she caught Grandmother's eye. The old lady nodded. "Lina's right. The goddesses will guide her and keep us safe." She turned to Angelina. "Deal. Howl when you've killed them. We'll listen for the howl and we'll find you. Now, tell us how you're going to tempt them here."

"I'm working on it."

The social grapevine revealed that the weekend before Samhain the brothers would be attending a masked soirée in the exclusive nightclub, 'Puck's Playground.'

Old Margie's sewing machine produced a silk, rhinestone-encrusted mask that apart from the eyeholes would cover the upper half of Angelina's face; young Sophie's wardrobe provided a backless, almost frontless, crimson dress, suitable for the venue; and the Corsa was ready and waiting.

Angelina had one concern. She confided in Grandmother. "If the brothers are masked I may find it difficult to recognise them."

Grandmother said, "You may, but the wolf won't. She'll remember their father and grandfather's scent and she'll recognise a similarity in the boys'. Although you'll be in human form she's still part of you. Access her senses. Practise until it comes easily to you."

Grandmother was right, as usual. She practised and the wolf co-operated.

The weekend before Samhain Angelina drove to 'Puck's Playground' and tucked the Corsa in a dark corner of the car park. She donned her mask and joined society's finest, who were strutting, swaying and throwing shapes on the dance floor.

Using the wolf's senses she located the brothers. Chiron appeared to be floating in the ether on a comforting hallucinogenic cloud. No point bothering with him. He wouldn't be capable of taking the bait she was about to set. Demetrius was observing the proceedings with cynical amusement. His attention was on a young woman who was wearing a dress held together by clothes pegs. Keeping out of his line of sight, Angelina circled the 'Playground' and approached him from behind. Laying a hand on his shoulder, she whispered into his ear, "A witch will lurk in Brechfa Forest on the night the full moon rises. You'll find her by the ancient oak tree."

He reached out to grab her wrist but she dodged him and melted back into the whooping, grinning gaggle of the nation's darlings.

She escaped into the fresh night air and took a deep breath before starting her journey home.

On her twentieth birthday, the night of the full moon, she hid close to the ancient oak and she waited. She saw the brothers approach. They were each holding a knife. She freed the wolf and leaped upon Demetrius, sinking her fangs into his neck. Chiron dropped his knife and ran, screaming into the forest.

Leaving Demetrius whimpering as he bled to death, she bounded after his brother and found him sprawled in the tangled vegetation, his ankle lying at an awkward angle. He was pointing a gun at her.

Time slowed down. Was this how it would end? The silver bullet nonsense was dreamed up in the eighteenth century. Whatever the metal of Chiron's choice, she'd be just as dead when he fired it. The witches would hear it. They'd come to find her and he'd kill them too. She'd failed them and she'd failed her mother.

A flicker of movement in the undergrowth caught her eye. The shadow sprang, knocking the gun from Chiron's hand.

She shouted, mind to mind at the towering grey wolf, "Who are you?"

"I'm your father. Deal with this wretch as you must, Angelina. Then we will speak."

Her father? Why hadn't he told her before now? Typical male. Can't do anything without drama.

She turned back to the wretch, who pleaded, "Please don't kill me. If this is because of the witch, I didn't burn her. They made me watch."

He disgusted her but she didn't sense in him the evil viciousness of the other three Finders. She would be merciful. She ripped out his throat and he died instantly.

It was done. She howled, to signal the witches. They'd hear her. They'd find her and take Chiron's body. The brothers would be burned and sacrificed to Hekate.

She returned to human form. Tears that she'd held back for years filled her eyes. She cried for her mother, for the lost years they should have had together and for the way she met her death.

The grey wolf said, "I hoped you'd choose to be a wolf and join me in the forest, but I see that you're human. Wolves don't cry. Only humans cry."

She turned to him. "I'm both. Are you?"

"I once was, but I chose to be the wolf. If you ever make that choice I'll be waiting." He slipped into the shadows and the forest took him back.

The witches approached. Grandmother handed Angelina a bathrobe and hugged her while her companions dragged Chiron's body back to the clearing. She said, "Dry your tears, Lina, and join us in welcoming Samhain. The veil between the worlds of the living and the dead will grow thin and your mother will be near."

They returned to the clearing and they burned the brothers' bodies. Matthew Hopkins's bloodline became extinct.

At midnight the witches sang a welcome to Samhain. The air shimmered and the veil parted. Angelina's mother stepped through. She said, "You've done well. Lina. You met the challenge to destroy the Finders and you succeeded. Now you must bond with your father."

Although he'd saved her life, Angelina felt a stab of anger against the grey wolf. "He shouldn't have left us. Why did he do that?"

"Don't be angry with him, child. He was a good man; a gentle man with a noble heart. He loved us both and I loved him but I couldn't hold him against Selene's wishes. He had to leave. The call of the forest was too strong."

"He wants me to join him. I don't know which choice to make: to be human or wolf."

Her mother smiled. "There is a third choice. You can be both. You have a dual identity and you don't have to sacrifice it."

Angelina said, "The choice I would make if I could is to be with you again."

"We will be together. When the time comes you'll pass through the veil, but first   you have a life to live. Accept it, live it well and be happy. If Selene allows it, your father may regain his dual identity through knowing you, and one day you'll both join me." She raised her hand in farewell, retreated from the world of the living and the veil closed,

Angelina's spirits lifted. She knew what she needed to do.

Also by Maureen Bowden:

Whispers of Magic

Legends and unusual characters abound in England, where you never know who or what you might meet in the forests. Maureen Bowden introduces you to them in these stories of magic and misdirection...and

https://www.hiraethsffh.com/product-page/whispers-of-magic

The Oculist's Daughter
By Angel Favazza

The Oculist's Daughter by Angel Favazza is a steampunker in the old west. It's got a semi-mad scientist (her dad), her, of course, plus outlaws, Indians, Wyoming, a poison gas for killing natives, and an Indian guide. It all adds up to a rollicking adventure.

https://www.hiraethsffh.com/product-page/oculist-s-daughter-by-angel-favazza

The Ugly Fairy
Matias Travieso-Diaz

*Someday you will be old enough
to start reading fairy tales again.*
C. S. Lewis, *The Lion, the Witch and the Wardrobe*

Florandel became convinced she was the ugliest fairy in the world. This was perhaps an unusual concern, for fairies are hazy, shapeless clouds of diffuse matter with just a small, better-defined nucleus where their essence resides. They lack any color and resemble pulsating, featureless bursts of gas. Yet, once Earth became ruled by humans, fairies found the need to interact with the smart apes and began to assume more distinct shapes that would be pleasing to the men and women with whom they dealt.

Her doubts about her appearance arose one spring morning when, as the mists dissipated, Florandel was hovering over a field of just opened roses and admiring their delicate shapes and aromas when a human girl, barely five or six years old, came out of her dwelling holding a watering can and stationed herself in front of the flower patch. She was beginning to sprinkle water on the roses when she noticed Florandel, shrieked, and ran back home.

Florandel became upset at the incident. Traditionally, in areas populated by humans, a fairy would make itself appear small and not intimidating; it would mask its shimmering nature by adopting a delicate form along the lines of that of a human female clad in transparent, flowing robes, and appeared endowed with large, colorful wings that made the fairy more pleasing to the human eye.

What went wrong? worried Florandel. *Is there something about me that draws humans away?* She floated over to the stream that ran by the woods, gazed at her "human" image in the clear waters, and compared it to the looks of other fairies. After long consideration, the fairy concluded that her looks were deficient. Her ears seemed unusually large, her nose a bit crooked, her skin somewhat bluish instead of the pearly white displayed by other fairies. Since she looked different than the other fairies and they were accepted by the humans she, Florandel, must be ugly.

Florandel and a group of other fairies dwelt in a vast forest, having only limited contact with each other and with the human population. The fairies, however, gathered occasionally to consult about matters felt to be significant. In those encounters, they often took counsel from one fairy, wiser perhaps than the rest, Gloriana, whose advice was almost invariably followed.

It was to Gloriana that Florandel carried the misgivings about her appearance. As they met in Gloriana's underground dwelling, the sage listened attentively to Florandel's tiny energy discharges that serve for words among the fairy folk. Gloriana was bemused: "Your concerns are unfounded. You can assume any appearance you choose, and can be as fair as you desire, and as beautiful – however you measure it – as any of your sisters."

"Not so, Mother," replied Florandel, utilizing the form of address that the fairies in this community chose when "speaking" to Gloriana. "As you know, we fairies must adopt a certain appearance when making ourselves visible to humans. This appearance may vary depending on the skills and physical characteristics of each one of us. Thus, we all appear to a human as if we have a face with eyes and a nose and a mouth, and limbs and a body, but what they see when they look at us may be different for each fairy. I just experienced that, when a human of tender years looked at me, her face became distorted in disgust or fear, and she ran away. However, I have observed how, when they see Oriande or Luminaria, young humans smile and their eyes widen with excitement."

"So, you are judging your beauty by the reaction of humans when they meet you?"

"We have no other standard by which to judge. Appearing before a horse or a rabbit yields no results."

"My daughter, there are two flaws in your self-evaluation. First, we cannot read the minds and feelings of humans, and therefore cannot use their facial expressions, or even their words or actions, as measures of the opinions they form of us. Second, and more important, you are letting the judgment of inferior beings be used to assess your worth. If you are really concerned about what you call your beauty, you need to measure it yourself."

"But how can I do that?"

"It so happens that the issue has come up before, in another situation. Let me show you something." Gloriana glided to a dark corner of the cave and returned holding a thin gold necklace from which hung twenty-eight bezel-set colorless gemstones. "Put this around what, in your human form, would be your neck, and wear it continuously through one complete cycle of the moon."

"What does it do?"

"Each morning, as the moon sets, one of the gemstones in this necklace may become shiny like a diamond or turn dark red like a ruby, or maybe none will change. At the end of the twenty-eighth day, look at your reflection on the stream that runs past the waterfall east of here. The image that you see will be your true self, and you will be able to determine whether you are indeed beautiful or ugly."

"What does the coloring of the gemstones mean?"

"A gemstone turning bright like a diamond means that you have become more beautiful than the previous day. One gemstone turning dark red warns that your beauty has decreased. A day in which no gemstone changes color your beauty has remained the same."

"Do I have to wait a full lunar month before I can learn the results?"

"You can gaze at your image on the stream as often as you wish, but the true result, containing the necklace's final judgment on your beauty, will only be reached on the final day."

"Seems like a cumbersome way of finding out what a mere glance should reveal."

"You would be surprised how much true beauty depends on things that can change in very short order. In any event, this method is a far more accurate way of discovering a fairy's beauty than relying on the reactions of humans."

***

That afternoon, as Florandel was making her rounds of the border between the forest and the adjoining human settlements, her attention was caught by cries arising from a hollow in the terrain. Approaching, the fairy noticed that a fawn had been caught in a snare and was wailing in pain. Floarandel moved swiftly to force the snare open and rescue the animal, which limped away, bleating to evince relief, or perhaps to give thanks to the fairy for its rescue.

Nothing else of any significance happened that day, but the following morning as she bent over the clear waters of the stream, Florandel noticed that her ears, which heretofore had been – in her estimation – too large, appeared to have shrunk slightly. Also, one of the gemstones hanging from the necklace was shining brightly.

***

The second day went by without incident, and there were no changes in the fairy's reflected appearance or the necklace's condition. On the third day, however, Florandel ran into a gaggle of boys who were playing wheelbarrow races near one of the farms. The children were so intent in their play that they did not notice the presence of the fairy, which suddenly felt a bit upset at being ignored. Florandel turned herself into a hummingbird, an eye-catching metallic green speck of feathers with a bright red throat, and began whirring its wings rapidly as it flew above the heads of the children.

Several of the children were drawn to give chase to the bird, who would fly tantalizingly close and then move away just enough to let them come near and almost touch it. The chase went on for quite a while, with Florandel luring the kids farther and farther into the forest. After a while, the chasers got tired and began dropping out of the

23

pursuit, but one towheaded, freckled faced seven-year-old persisted and went on and on, chasing the elusive bird, until they reached a remote corner of the woods. There, the hummingbird hung high in the air, forcing the boy to stop. He then realized, for the first time, he was in totally unfamiliar surroundings and had become lost.

Florandel's initial impulse was to guide the boy back to safety, but then the fairy reflected: "Boys should learn not to chase after little creatures and possibly harm them." She flew away, leaving the boy alone. He became increasingly afraid as the afternoon wore on and night approached.

The fairy came back hours later and, after some searching, found the boy sitting on a fallen log, whimpering disconsolately. She realized the prank had gone a bit too far and, changing back into a human-like appearance, approached the terrified child and greeted him: "What are you doing, young man, sitting by yourself in the dark?"

The boy was too scared to answer, and Florandel asked again: "Would you like to go home?" This time, the boy managed to reply haltingly: "Yee... ah, ye...aah, pleeease!!"

Florandel led the boy back to the meadow where they had first met. It was later discovered that he had developed a permanent stutter.

Florandel also learned, the morning after this encounter, that one of the necklace's gems had turned dark red, her ears had gone back to appearing unusually large, and her nose was more crooked.

***

The days advanced in quick succession, sometimes holding new adventures, others passing uneventfully. Florandel had several opportunities to be helpful to humans and beasts, extricating a cart stranded in the mud, shining a guiding light that allowed a traveler to find his way out of the forest, leaving a pot of fresh milk at the door of an elderly couple, guarding a sparrow's nest against a marauding murder of crows. The fairy was also mischievous from time to time, pinching cows to set a stampede that interrupted their grazing, luring a passerby into an elaborate maze where he would linger for hours, imitating the growls of ferocious animals to scare hunters away, stealing eggs from a chicken coop and pies left on a window to cool.

At the end of the lunar month, Florandel's enchanted necklace sported over a dozen sparkling diamonds, seven dark stones, and some dull, colorless gems. As for the fairy's reflection on the stream, some aspects of her looks had improved: the eyes now shone bright green, the curvature of the lips was more perfect, the hair shone like gold. On the other hand, the ears were now longer, the nose more aquiline, and the skin had acquired more of a bluish tinge than the hue Florandel favored. Overall, the changes did little to alter the overall balance of the fairy's human appearance, which seemed to be sort of pretty, but not outstanding.

Bitterly disappointed, the fairy paid another visit to Gloriana's cave. "Look at me!" Florandel complained. "This necklace is worthless! The image of me it shows is almost the same that humans see! Am I that ugly?"

Gloriana smiled. "Perhaps your true inner being is not that different from the outer image humans perceive when they look at you. Do not blame the necklace, for it is not meant to improve your appearance but reflect your true self. The colors of the gemstones in the necklace reflect your character. You tend to be helpful and compassionate, but at the same time cannot resist performing pranks that are hurtful to others. You are like all creatures, a mixture of good, bad, and indifferent. Be thankful that the good predominates, and that on balance you make a positive contribution to the order of things."

"But..."

"No more buts. Lead your life the best you can, and your true beauty will shine through."

"I don't want to be better, just more beautiful."

"Sorry about that. You are beautiful enough as it is. Now be gone!"

And Florandel realized it was time to accept her looks, such as they were, and disappeared in a cloud of mist to float around the forest.

Eadon
Lee Clark Zumpe

It's said Echu Tirmcharna, king of Connacht,
and great-great grandson of Dauí Tenga Uma,
encountered you on Brí Léith,
just this side of the Otherworld,
dutifully washing from a silver vessel
alongside the edge of a well.
In retrospect, his enthusiasm seems suspect.

When Midir of the Tuatha Dé Danann
took you as his wife, jealous Fúamnach
orchestrated a sorcerous response,
transforming you into a scarlet fly;
rebirth did not improve your fortune –
Midir reclaimed you in a game of chance,
as if your affection was a reasonable payout.

I wonder if I might find you there,
celebrating Lughnasa at the base of Brí Léith,
or wandering the streets of nearby Ardagh
carrying a bucket of bilberries;
I wonder if you still visit the Otherworld,
call on the Tuatha Dé Danann,
and inspire dreaming poets.

let there be worlds aplenty
Lee Clark Zumpe

let there be worlds aplenty,
full of vistas undreamt,
shorelines uncharted,
landscapes untamed,
and fantastical cities unvisited –
all yearning for discovery
beyond the wall of sleep,
amidst the invented provinces
scattered across our imagination.

let there be worlds aplenty,
full of sites so extraordinary,
spectacles so unfamiliar,
topography so strange,
and civilizations so alien –
all yearning for discovery
across the Milky Way,
and amidst countless galaxies
scattered across the cosmos.

Also by Lee Clark Zumpe:

Wearing Winter Gray

Atmospheric poetry at its finest is found in Wearing Winter Gray. Lee Clark Zumpe sets his moods and draws forth evocative images and memories, and not a little emotion. Now and then a ray of light shines through his words, so that having created a somber mood, he punctuates it with a bit of joy. Thus it is that Wearing Winter Gray reminds us that Shiny Summer Colors are just around the corner.

Print: https://www.hiraethsffh.com/product-page/wearing-winter-gray-by-lee-clark-zumpe
ePub: https://www.hiraethsffh.com/product-page/wearing-winter-gray-by-lee-clark-zumpe-2
PDF: https://www.hiraethsffh.com/product-page/wearing-winter-gray-by-lee-clark-zumpe-1

Rover

Gustavo Bondoni

"Mom!" Lara yelled. "Rover's gone!"

"You should have left him in orbit like I told you to," I replied, suppressing a sigh.

"We need to go find him."

"He'll be back."

"How do you know? We just got him. We don't know if he can make it back."

I sighed. This could only end one way, and both of us knew it. Lara, at four, was of the age where she believed volume and single-mindedness could overcome any logical argument. I pressed the intercom button. "Geno?" I said. "How's that coming?"

"Nearly done."

"All right. We'll need to do an EVA soon. The rover went missing."

"Ugh. All right. Give me ten minutes. I'll meet you in the locker," he replied.

"Can you send Mariah to take care of Lara while we're out?"

"She'll be pissed."

I laughed. Men were helpless around children, no matter what age. "She's sixteen. She's always pissed. Just get her to come over here."

Mariah arrived, I handed Lara off to her and headed to the suit locker.

***

The surface of Titan wasn't as dangerous as other places in the Solar System. Sure, you couldn't breathe the air, and you needed powerful lights to see under the cloud layer, and you needed to be well-shielded from the radiation. But there was an actual atmosphere—mostly nitrogen—and the pressure meant that a leak in your suit wouldn't cause an explosive depressurization. If you did pick up a rip, you were actually in more danger from the cold.

In fact, the extreme cold was the reason we'd decided to make a stop at Titan. It was a great place to fill a few tanks with liquid hydrocarbons, including liquid methane.

"There are the tracks," Geno said, pointing at two parallel lines a little over a foot apart, that disappeared into the distance.

"Yeah. Straight into the lake basin, of course."

"Of course." He laughed, resignedly. We'd been parents long enough that we laughed resignedly at everything from spills to hairline hull fissures caused by tantrum-impelled objects hitting the side of a spacecraft.

A missing pet, brought to the surface of a planet because a child couldn't bear to leave it on the ship, was just another day in the life.

"Wow," I said, looking into the depths of a lake that, before the great exodus, had been large and deep. "This was a big one."

"And to think they probably drained it in a single operation. They probably thought one less methane lake on Titan was a small price to pay for one ship to the stars," he replied.

"It's still beautiful, even without the lakes," I replied.

It was. The basin, exposed by our helmet-mounted floodlights, reminded me of the amphitheater in Polis Mars, except that the people watching the any play in this place would have been giants a hundred feet tall, colossal beings made possible by gravity a fraction of that on Mars, and much less than Earth. Even Earth's moon had a stronger pull than Titan.

"What made Rover take off, anyway?" Geno asked.

"I have no idea," I replied.

Even though he was behind me, I could imagine Geno rolling his eyes. I didn't even need to see it to know it was happening. "So you never checked its origin and programming." It wasn't a question.

"Well, I saw it was rated safe for co-inhabiting human spaces, including child-safety protocols and I was going to check its main programming, but then we had the hydroponics line burst and Mari was sick and... well, and then we had to do the burn to enter orbit here and prep the lander habitat and..."

"And..." he repeated. As usual, he was more amused than angry. "I'm betting Rover is programmed to locate liquid hydrocarbons on the surface for the suction tubes. Except he was never deployed once the big lakes on Titan were sucked dry. He and all his little wheeled friends were probably abandoned once the ships began refining the methane out of Jupiter's atmosphere. No need to stop in the Saturn system anymore after that."

"You miss them? The ships?" I said.

"You know me better than that," he replied, still amused.

Yeah, I did. We'd made a good living servicing the big monsters, the hollowed-out asteroids that carried hundreds of thousands of colonists and scooped up every useful raw material in their wake. But the life we'd found after they left, the life of living by our own rules in scattered communities that existed in and around the abandoned infrastructure, the endless refueling stations and factory facilities with entire worlds to call their own among the moons and moonlets of Saturn... was a freedom unlike anything any other community had ever had. Even the people in the Asteroid Belt were packed tighter than we were.

I turned on the helmet audio, to listen to our footsteps. With the low clouds and the huge, bowl-shaped depression, I felt they should be echoing loudly, but other than the crunch of regolith mixed with ice crystals, I heard nothing.

"He went around that rock formation over there. I bet his sensors detected methane on the wind and his programming just took over," Geno said. He loved trying to solve technical mysteries. He'd often spend hours on the stations we docked at searching for malfunctions he could set right, not because they were important, but because it amused him much more than the infinite library of content ceaselessly beamed up from Earth and Mars.

"Shouldn't we turn back?" I said.

"No need. We've been walking for ten minutes, and we have air for four hours. We're good."

"I just don't like the slope we just climbed down."

He looked back. "Yeah. I can understand that. But in this gravity, it's barely even a slope."

I wasn't sure about that. If we'd been in the hab, I'd have sat down with a pencil and figured whether the low gravity was doing us any favors or actually messing up our friction factors so we'd be unable to get any grip on the climb back up. But I didn't say anything: I knew if I did, I'd have to listen to him go on about it until we got back.

I chuckled at the thought, but not on the open comm.

"So what is it about this rover that made Lara fall in love with it?" he said.

"Oh, I dumped the dog program into it. It followed Lara around the entire time we were on L17 station."

"Do we really need another rover on the ship? It's always the same. The kids get tired of them, the batteries wear out and we can't throw them out, because the kids won't let us."

"If we could spend some more time in one of the larger settlements, where she could be with kids her own age.... And Mariah really needs a social life. She can't keep her friends through the Mindnet alone."

Geno sighed. I knew he hated having anything to do with the pockets of population scattered around the Saturn system. But we both knew I was right, so I insisted.

"It doesn't have to be the Enceladus dome. We can spend a few months at Freighterville."

"I guess," he said. "I know I've been putting it off. But now she's four, I guess we should let her have some schooling."

"And Mariah's sixteen. She needs to be with people her age."

"I thi—" the word cut off midway and he disappeared from view.

A moment later, I felt the ground below my boots shift unexpectedly.

Then, I was falling. I landed on Geno.

"Oof!"

"Sorry about that," I said. "Are you all right?"

"Yes, fine," he said.

There was something in his voice... "What's wrong?"

"Crack in my wrist joint."

For a second, I thought he'd hurt his actual body, and was about to tell him it was nothing... then I realized he was talking about his suit. "I think I have some sealant," I replied.

"You brought sealant? On a walk to grab a rover?"

"Of course. Never leave the hab without it."

"Sheesh," he said. Annoyed even though my OCD would keep him alive. For a while longer, at least.

I applied the heated goo to the crack. It wasn't a small one, but I got it sealed up. "We need to head back now," I said.

"Any ideas on how to get out of this hole? I don't think we can climb these walls—they're too loosely-packed," he said. "These lake beds where they pulled out all the methane are no good to climb. They still have crystals from frozen material the ships didn't take. Water and stuff."

"We could call Mariah. She can throw down a rope," I said.

"You think that's safe? For her, I mean."

"Safer than she'll be trying to fly the hab lander back to the main ship in orbit if we die out here."

Geno got on the comm. "Mariah, can you hear us? If you can, will you answer? This is your father." He paused for ten seconds, then tried again. "Mariah?"

"Damn," he said to me. "She's not answering. Probably got the music up too high."

"The signal is probably too weak to reach her," I said. "Give her a break."

He grunted. "I'm activating the emergency beacon on my suit. Do the same. Those are more powerful than the comm."

"Battery life..."

"Is irrelevant at this point. The juice will last eight hours even with the beacon at full strength. We've got four hours of air. Besides..."

"What?"

"Nothing."

"What is it?"

"Suit temp is starting to drop. I think I have three hours before it gets really chilly in here."

Suits didn't use heaters. They were so well-insulated that the problem was more one of radiating out excess heat from our own bodies inside without overdoing it and freezing us. It was a delicate balance.

"We should at least try to climb out. Do you think you could throw me to the top?" The ledge was five or six body-lengths overhead, but in this gravity, it might just be possible.

He looked up. "We can try."

Geno cupped his hands together and held them out. I stood on his hands, bent my knees and jumped as he pushed me up.

The angle was perfect, the distance was there, and I reached the edge of the wall, right at the very top.

I got my arms up and scrambled, trying to get my weight over the edge.

The regolith crumbled and slowly, so slowly, I fell back into Geno's waiting arms.

He looked into my eyes through the visor.

"I love you," he said.

I knew there was something seriously wrong. I checked his wrist. The crack had grown, expelling part of the sealant. It must have happened when he threw me upwards. Was his skin getting hit by the full brunt of the exterior temperature, just 94K?

I rummaged around inside the suit pocket and pulled out another tube of sealant. I worked desperately to get it into the break, to get every crack covered with goo before the cold hardened it.

Geno shook his hands a couple of times to check my work, then sat on an outcropping and laughed.

"What?" I said.

"You brought two of them," he said.

"Three," I replied. "One for each of us... and a spare, just in case."

His visor turned my way. "I do love you, you know."

"You're just saying that because I saved your life again."

"No," his voice was suddenly serious. "I'm saying it because I might not have the chance to do so ever again. I don't trust the beacon this deep in the hole. I want to try throwing you up there again."

"No."

"There might not be anyone coming for us," he insisted.

"Then we'll wait here until time becomes an issue. I'm not risking that wrist breaking open and killing you."

He didn't like it. I could tell by the way he slumped back. But I didn't care. "Do you still love me?"

"Of course," he replied.

That scared me. It wasn't like him to avoid an argument... he really was frightened.

We talked as we waited. An hour passed, and we reminisced about how we'd started out with nothing. Twenty-year-olds on a five-year contract, married but forbidden from having kids. How we moved up in seniority because we were good at what we did, until the company tore up the contract and offered us pay-employee status.

How we conceived Mariah that very night and nearly lost our contracts, but proved we were worth keeping on. And how we'd come to love the stark, dangerous emptiness between the worlds, the stale air of cramped stations and the bright pinprick of stars.

"We've had a good life," he said. "Didn't we?"

"We're not dead yet."

"I've got about forty minutes before I freeze," he said. "Will you let me throw you, now?"

I cried silently for two minutes until I noticed beeping sound in my helmet.

"What the hell is that?" I asked, suddenly excited.

"Some automated robot transmission," Geno replied. "Probably one of the old pumping stations they used to empty this moon of anything they could use. Likely interrogating our beacon."

"No. Wait. I know that pattern." I opened a channel. "Rover?"

"Affirmative. Unit 45-24-C responding to distress signal. How can I assist?"

"Do you have a rope?"

"Negative."

"Damn," Geno said. "And how long would you take to get back to the hab from here?"

"I estimate thirty-seven minutes," the rover replied.

"Good," Geno replied. "Go get Mariah. Inform her of our position and tell her to bring a rope."

"No!" I yelled. "You won't make it."

"But you will," he replied.

"Screw that. Rover."

"Yes?"

"Can you relay my radio to the hab?"

"Affirmative."

"Please do."

"Comm established."

"Mariah," I said.

"Mom! I'm scared, where are you?"

"The rover will send you coordinates. Get suited up and bring a rope and a deep anchor for fine regolith. And be careful with the ground. Check for crevices with your suit radar. Run, now."

"Are you all right?"

"We're fine, but you need to run. Explain to Lara that you'll be back in a few minutes."

I don't know how she did it, but that girl reached us in fifteen minutes flat, and had her father out of the hole in another five. Then the rope came back and she pulled me out.

"Where's your father?" I said.

She shook her head. "He said he had to run, that he was seriously cold and had to hurry."

Had he lied to me again? Just to make me relax? Did he actually have less time than he told me? It would be just like him.

We walked back, the rover in tow. I'd overridden its primary programming which, as Geno had suspected, was to search for liquid hydrocarbons.

When the hab came into view and I saw Geno walking around inside with Lara in his arms, I broke down and cried.

***

"So where now?" I asked Geno.

We sat in the galley of our main ship, the Open Spaces. The remains of dinner, reconstituted partly from the hydrocarbons we'd brought from Titan by mining pockets too small for the colony ships to bother with, sat on the table.

He looked around the table. "The Enceladus Dome."

Mariah's face brightened. "What? But dad, you hate that place. You aren't messing with me, are you?"

Geno shook his head.

"Lara needs to go to school," I explained. "She needs to be with kids her age and..."

"That's not it," Geno interrupted. "Or, that's only part of it." He looked at Mariah. "I just realized that we're being unfair to you. You've wanted to spend time there forever. And we said no, because you were just a kid and we knew better." He wiped his eye. "But I saw a young woman out there who did better than any adult I know, including her parents. So I'm asking you where you want to go. Of course, if you don't want to go to Enceladus..."

"You're kidding, right?" Mariah said.

"Then, Enceladus it is."

37

Mariah leaped across the table and hugged her father the way she used to when she was five, the way she never did anymore.

And I found myself tearing up again.

Starwinders: Nohana's Heart

The scion of a corporate hierarch, Angrboda Vigdisdottir (Ayvy) wants to hijack a gold shipment to prevent an interstellar war. Disgraced security operative Pol Cahill is the ideal partner for her, given his skill set. Unfortunately, personalities clash. Finally, on a remote world, the two encounter one another in a tavern, and find that a young woman named Nohana, intensely educated and with a desire to travel among the stars, takes to the pair.

But the personalities continue to clash even as plans are laid to steal the gold. Nohana fills the power vacuum and becomes the so-called adult in the room. But Cahill is shot and wounded before they can carry out their plan. Nohana now has no choice but to try to save the day, despite her lack of experience. Meanwhile, the war awaits.

Ordering links:
Print: https://www.hiraethsffh.com/product-page/starwinders-nohana-s-heart-by-tyree-campbell

PDF: https://www.hiraethsffh.com/product-page/starwinders-1-nohana-s-heart-by-tyree-campbell

ePub: https://www.hiraethsffh.com/product-page/starwinders-1-nohana-s-heart-by-tyree-campbell-1

Shoebox
Sandra Siegienski

It was the argument with Carl that started the whole thing. He was one of those rugged, independent types who generally preferred motorcycles to other people, but he had a soft spot in his heart for Marti, and he'd been her boyfriend for almost a year.

"You should think about getting out more," he suggested that evening over dinner.

Marti had heard this before. Uneasiness grew in the pit of her stomach. She couldn't explain. Carl would never understand. He was fearless. "I guess I'm allergic to public proximity," she cheerfully retorted. Too bad magic spells didn't exist for her.

"You won't even go out to dinner with me," he said, clearly frustrated. They were eating leftover rotisserie chicken and wilted salad for the second day in a row. Marti hadn't been able to face the grocery store, and Carl had been too busy to shop. "Your life's becoming a shoebox."

"Hey! Low blow." Marti chucked a wadded-up paper towel ball at his head. It bounced off and landed in the sink. "You know I don't like crowds."

"I get it. But you're not a turtle. You can't stay in the house *all* the time."

"I like it here." Marti perched nervously on the edge of her chair. She wasn't about to admit the extent of the problem. Carl was too close to the truth.

"I'd like your company out there."

Marti hesitated. The awkward pause grew, and grew. Her face reddened.

Finally, Carl shoved his chair back. "Fine. If the shoebox fits, wear it!"

Last month, when Marti's Uncle Owen had visited, he'd used that annoying phrase way too often. Carl had unfortunately picked it up.

Marti tried to explain, "This is the only place I feel safe. I'm actually comfortable in my own home. Can't you understand that?" She loved dinners with Carl, even if the food left something to be desired. But unfortunately, restaurants—and stores—just had too many *people*. She wanted a shell of invisibility, or *something*.

"Then maybe you should take it with you." Carl got up, grabbed his leather jacket, and shrugged himself into it. "Babe, there's an exciting world out there, and someday I'd like to share it with you. But I guess that's not gonna happen anytime soon."

She stared at his handsome face, the concern in his eyes, the sadness at the corners of his mouth. Was he leaving her? Her mind raced and her heart started pounding—that awful, familiar pounding. Embarrassment burned in her face and, desperate, she searched for words that would bring Carl back.

Nothing came.

Sighing, he walked out the front door. The screen door slammed with finality.

Marti sat alone and wordless, torn in half and hating every minute of it.

Carl had always assumed she was an independent loner, like him. Now, despite her best attempts at cover-up, he'd uncovered her secret.

She was afraid of the world.

It wasn't that Carl was unsympathetic, but she did stay at home, working online for Pixie Products, imagining what she could do with her life...but too afraid of public places, open spaces, and people to step out. She'd tried everything: counseling, groups, animal therapy.... Nothing seemed to work.

She didn't want to lose Carl. And she wanted to be out there enjoying life like everyone else.

All four walls of her empty house seemed to stare down on her scathingly as if she had driven out the best thing in their collective flat lives.

She cried. A good wallow in self-pity never hurt anyone. Then, she dried her face and gave the walls a hard look. A solution lay in this misery somewhere. She'd take half a solution. It was the twenty-first century, for cripes sake, and people had brains.

"Okay," she said to Carl's long-gone back. "I'll take it with me."

*   *   *

Marti stayed up all night working, so caught up in her idea that she couldn't sleep. Maybe the bags under her eyes wouldn't show. It shouldn't matter, if her plan worked.

It was an original solution. Even Uncle Owen couldn't argue with that.

When Marti finished with her cutting, sewing, hammering, and trimming, she had a five-foot-one-inch-tall shoebox, neatly fitted to her body size. The blue and ivory stretch-fabric sides had carefully designed holes for her arms. The open base let her walk. It covered her head, with a large face hole easy see through, the edges delicately lined with a silk fringe matching her color scheme.

She examined the results in the mirror on the living room wall and turned a circle in satisfaction. Sitting was a little awkward, and driving like this would take some adjustment. Walking was fine, though. "I need to take this on the road. Maybe a short excursion, first time out."

WallShop should be pretty safe. Besides, she needed something to match her outfit. *Maybe new socks.*

It was an easy eight blocks on a fine autumn day. Perfect for a new start. With a last glance in the mirror, Marti grabbed her purse, took a deep breath, and headed to the front door. Would this work? At the threshold, her heart once again started its familiar pounding in her ears, echoing inside her new shoebox and reminding her of all her fears.

She had to do this. *If the shoebox fits....*

Blast Uncle Owen. Maybe for once he'd actually helped. "To hell with it," she said to the door. "The shoebox fits fine, and I'm gonna wear it."

She opened the door. *Now or never...*

...and stepped over the threshold, awaiting the overwhelming panic she always dreaded.

Nothing happened.

She gripped her shoebox sides and slowly crossed the porch.

Nothing.

She relaxed, just a little. She hadn't felt this comfortable in years. Stepping down to the sidewalk, she gazed at the bright morning. No clouds in the sky. No people around. Just a broad, terrifying world in which to test her new attempt at life. It was both exhilarating and nerve-wracking.

Feeling out her outfit's idiosyncrasies, she walked to the mailbox. Not a twinge of anxiety. "Huh."

This thing was actually a success? "That's one step in the right direction." She laughed out loud, relief making her sag against the mailbox.

Next test: to see how she felt around crowds. "Let's do this!" she announced to nobody, then headed for WallShop. "I've missed enough of life."

*　*　*

Marti had trouble getting through the turnstile at WallShop, but it wasn't insurmountable. Turning sideways and bending her knees helped. Nobody seemed to notice. They were used to unusual things here.

Ordinarily, she was so panic-stricken out in public that she never noticed what was or wasn't normal at WallShop, but her new outfit was working fine. The thin, semi-flexible walls of the box were roomy enough not to make her feel claustrophobic, yet close enough that she could easily walk down aisles. Best of all, she had a sense of personal boundaries.

This is better than body armor, she thought. *And more comfortable.*

She headed confidently down aisle eleven, chose a pair of raspberry-colored socks, and went to the checkout counter. The teenage clerk with bright pink hair streaked with purple and sporting three nose-rings didn't even bat her theatrically made-up fluorescent green eyes when Marti casually leaned her new body-encasing, designer-fabric-decorated shoebox up against the counter.

She handed the socks to the clerk.

"On sale, fifty percent off the second pair, today," the girl announced. "You want another pair?"

"Not today, thanks. Maybe later." This was kind of fun. Maybe she should get more socks. What if she made another shoebox with different colors?

The clerk rang up the sale. "I just love your outfit. Nobody has any style anymore. I get *so* bored with everything." She waved her hand with its violet nail polish and multiple rings at the whole world.

"I know what you mean," Marti said, even though she didn't really, but who cared? For the first time in years, she was enjoying being out in public—despite the occasional blank stares she was getting. For once, her terror of the world wasn't ruining her day...yet. Maybe she'd try bowling next. She hadn't been to the alley in ten years, and Carl loved bowling.

* * *

Bowling was tricky, Marti found. She couldn't bend well, although she could hold a ball easily. Miniature golf was fine, however. Once back home, she discovered that gardening got the box dirty too fast, and the fabric soaked easily.

I'll use vinyl for an outdoor model, she thought, hosing off her shoes. *But I did it.* She felt inexpressibly proud of herself. She also needed a break before venturing out again. Rediscovering the world took energy.

Two days passed. Marti started on a second, then a third shoebox. Carl hadn't returned, but his things were all still in the house except for a few pairs of jeans, shirts, and his shaving kit. Marti's anxiety burgeoned. Their relationship might be over, but if it was, it wouldn't be because she hadn't left the house.

* * *

Marti's next excursion was to the dreaded grocery store, a place that often took her a week to summon up the courage to enter. She'd always envied the people who made shopping look easy.

Once inside Food-For-All, she grabbed a shopping basket, checking out the wide interior and high ceilings. Usually, it gave her the creeps.

44

"Marti! Is that you? You look lovely!" Her elderly neighbor approached, apparently drawn by the subtle luster of the brocade fabric on Marti's shoebox. The lady had a keen eye for detail.

"Hello, Mrs. Chang. It's me," Marti said, pleased. "It's something new I'm trying. But you'll have to excuse me, I'm in a rush. I can tell you about it tomorrow."

"Sure thing. It suits you well, dear. But then, you look lovely no matter what you wear."

"Oh, thank you!" Basking in the compliment but eager to finish her mission before her courage failed her, Marti ducked into the produce section, where she pretended to investigate organic broccoli while plotting her next move. Bagel chips? Opposite side of the store.

"Isn't that box adorable?" she overheard Mrs. Chang say. "Blue racing stripes on lilac, and that blush of peach near the top. Tasteful. I *must* ask her how she came up with that...."

"Magic," Marti whispered. This was way more fun than she'd expected.

"Can I help you find something, Ma'am?" a familiar male voice inquired behind her.

Carl!

Marti's mouth went dry. She quickly half-turned around, hoping to hide her face. Carl was holding a bag of chips, a rotisserie chicken, and a loaf of Italian bread. No cheese. He knew she didn't like cheese. What would he say if he recognized her? "Oh, dear me, no," she answered in her best fake falsetto English accent, trying not to let her voice quake, while pretending to fix her hair. "Thank you so much. Just browsing."

Carl didn't seem the slightest bit disturbed by the sight of a girl wearing a shoebox in the produce section. "All right. Just checking. You looked a little lost." He smiled at her, warm brown eyes and all.

She gave a little wave and ducked into the coffee aisle, giggling. *Of all the things that might save our relationship, maybe I've got the right one.*

*   *   *

That night, filled with success, Marti pored over patterns for shoebox designs. Other people out there had issues like hers. Would shoeboxes work for them, too?

A hand turned the front doorknob. She shot up from her chair.

Carl.

She hadn't changed out of her newest shoebox. She often wore one around the house because they were comfortable, like pajamas. Sometimes she forgot to take them off. Too late now. She held her breath as Carl walked in.

Seeing Marti encased in her jazzy gold-glitter shoebox, the first of her evening wear designs, his jaw dropped and he nearly let go of his sack of groceries. He set the bag down on the dining room table and leaned against the kitchen counter as if needing its help to stay upright while he scanned her from head to toe.

"Holy cow," he said. "I hadn't expected you'd take me seriously."

"What do you think?" Marti refused to quail at the moment of exposure. This was *herself* he was seeing. In a way. "The people at the golf course loved it and asked me to design one for them. I also joined an aikido class, but I have trouble with mobility. I'm working that out."

Carl whistled, staring at her. "You don't fool around."

Marti wished he would either kiss her, figure out something complimentary to say—and say it damn quick —or get out. "It wasn't something to fool around with."

Carl walked over and put his arm around her, shoebox and all. "I'm sorry I got so annoyed. It's just...."

"It was time for a change?" she finished for him. He kissed the top of her head, well, her shoebox, getting a little sparkle of glitter on his lips. She laughed. "I can get out of this." They could have one more fling and decide in the morning where they stood with each other.

He grinned. "I'll help you."

*   *   *

Marti and Carl agreed to give their relationship a month and then see how they felt about it. In the meantime, because of her growing feeling of distance from Carl, Marti decided to visit Uncle Owen and Aunt Gwen in uptown New York. She'd been terrified of public transportation but wanted to fly like everyone else.

"You'll be needing two seats?" asked her travel agent, his head bent close to his computer screen.

"I don't know." Marti had built her newest shoeboxes with flexible wire frames for easier sitting. They worked fine in the car, but she wasn't sure about a two-hour flight. It's be a good test for future travel models. "Yeah, let's go with that."

"Two it is," he agreed. "If in doubt, always get extra space. Keeps those energetic children and howling pets away from you."

Apprehensive but determined, Marti packed for the trip. Carl watched her from across the room. He hadn't quite gotten used to the change in her yet and she found this unsettling.

*   *   *

Marti arrived at the airport in good spirits, wearing her travel Shoebox, which was made of easy-wash stretch fabric in accordion fold pleats and accented with fine velvet shirrings to hide wrinkles. But, as she approached the terminal, with all those planes and huge concourses, twinges of the old, customary dread started surfacing. Her stomach tightened as she approached check-in.

Breathe!

She set her suitcase on the scale. The woman behind the counter glanced at her. "Overweight?"

"Me or the bag?" Marti asked.

"The bag."

"No."

She checked Marti's identification, tagged her bag, and sent her on without another word. Relief flooded Marti, but security screening was next. She stood in line, the other travelers eyeing her as she removed her shoes and emptied her flex-pockets. When her turn came to walk through the security scan, she took a deep breath and headed in, her stomach tied in knots.

Alarms went off.

Oh, damn. Marti's heart skipped. She felt her face pale. *What if I have to take off my shoebox?* The terminal suddenly loomed around her, overpowering.

The sixty-something security officer eyed her. "That's an interesting outfit, Ma'am. Would you step aside, please?"

Marti followed him, her heart pounding.

The officer wanded her all over. "Could you remove your hairclip, please?"

Metal. Oh, damn. She'd added the chunky accessory to hold back the silk curls adorning the top. "Sorry, I forgot." She handed it to him.

"Thank you. Now just go through again."

Holding her breath, Marti repeated her walk through security.

No alarm.

"Ok. You're fine. Here's your clip and other things. You have a safe trip."

Marti picked up her belongings, her racing heart settling down. "Thanks. I hope you have a good day."

"Always something interesting going on." The officer smiled at her and winked. "Love your outfit." He paused. "Say, do you sell outfits like that? I think I know someone who might like one. She's...kinda shy."

"I don't have much in stock because it's an experiment, but yeah, it's good for...shyness. And things. I'll get back to you."

After leaving security and pausing for a breath near the restrooms, the idea pursued Marti. Other people like her—and not like her—might very well enjoy her weird solution.

Anything was better than feeling trapped at home.

* * *

On board the plane, Marti's Shoebox neatly accommodated her window seat. She didn't need the second seat, although the comfort puppy of the passenger by the aisle gazed longingly at her fabric base as if dreaming of peeing on it. She gazed out the window as the jet accelerated for takeoff, triumphant that her horizons had broadened. She hoped her family would like the changes as much as she did.

*   *   *

"Holy crap!" Uncle Owen exclaimed as Marti ambled out the terminal door, heading for her relatives. "I like your style, girl!"

Pleased, she demurred, "It's just something I threw together. A new fashion statement." She would've blushed but no longer felt the need. *The end of false modesty.*

"You look amazing," Aunt Gwen gushed, hugging her carefully. "Can you show me the design? I love to sew."

"If the shoebox fits—" Uncle Owen began.

Aunt Gwen smacked him. "We got the idea."

The three of them spent an adventurous week trying everything from hiking to baseball. The only thing Marti had trouble doing in her shoebox was roller-skating. The acceptance she found in her relatives' hometown was astonishing. Outside of a few odd looks (which seemed directed at her old shoes—they didn't match her outfits or raspberry socks), no one acted surprised. On her flight home, despite lingering qualms, Marti decided it was time to find out if her own community would be as accepting.

Her out-of-town boost of confidence lasted until she left the airport. Once at home again, with Carl eyeballing her, the lingering old doubts rose up in her mind.

Recluse! they taunted. *Failure! You'll never have a real life.*

But I'm not a failure.

She'd had a great taste of life and wanted more. Time for higher stakes.

Marti shoved away her fears. She'd give her shoebox a try at the public library, where she used to read to the grade school kids in the after-school program. She always felt comfortable there, if nowhere else.

When she appeared at the library in her acid-washed, distressed-denim shoebox—which was decorated with tiny gold chains, tattoo-ish designs, and a few modest piercings—the kids crowded around her with the same enthusiasm as the WallShop clerk on her first day out.

49

"Can we sign our names?" asked an eager ten-year-old girl with a French braid. (Marti had added red braided silk to her shoebox top to match the latest hairstyles.) The possibility of signatures hadn't crossed her mind.

"Sure." She fished around in her purse and pulled out a pen and some bright markers. What better show of acceptance? "Sign anywhere you want on the lower sides, or up on the back. Oh, I like graffiti, too!"

"Cool!" The kids laughed and grabbed her markers. "Better than signing a cast," someone whispered. As they signed and drew, a stylish parent approached Marti, raising that familiar anxiety; perhaps the parents wouldn't quite understand.

"Hi, I'm Ava, Katie's mother." The woman indicated the girl with the French braid. "I just love what you're doing. It must be so empowering, and it makes such a compelling statement."

"Thank you," Marti said, floored. "I spent quite a while on the design." She didn't mention what had driven her to design it in the first place.

"I can tell." Ava's admiring glance swept over her with approval. "If you ever decide to go into business, there's a wide-open market out there."

"I was considering the idea, actually." Marti thought of the security officer's request at the airport. Ava did marketing and research, and she'd have good connections. "Can I get back to you?"

"Definitely." Ava smiled. "Get in touch with me, anytime. We can discuss marketing strategies." She handed Marti her card, then went back to her books and tablet.

"Excuse me...." Someone coughed politely behind Marti. She turned around to see the librarian, a nice guy in maybe his thirties—like her. His wildly curly hair framed a handsome face that spoke of long hikes in sunshine, and he held a sheaf of colorful printouts. He blushed, gazing at her. The kids grinned, moving aside to make room for him.

He said, "I couldn't help but admire your statement. May I say you look simply stunning? The cocoa top even matches your eyes."

Marti blinked, then smiled. "Oh, I…. Wow. Thanks." She hadn't spoken much with him before. Too stressed.

He proffered the printouts. "I saw you around town and noticed your design improvements. So, I looked up a few styles I thought might appeal to you."

She accepted the papers, enchanted that he'd taken such an interest. "I love this. Can we talk in a while? We'll be done with reading hour soon. Actually, I think it's turned into art hour."

The kids giggled, elbowing each other, sharing knowing looks.

"Anytime." The librarian's face lit up with his smile. He extended his hand. "I'm Kevin."

His warm handshake matched hers. "Kevin, I'm Marti, of Shoebox Designs."

*   *   *

That evening, Marti and Kevin met over a candlelit dinner (her newest shoebox included flame retardants and nonflammable materials), and together they pored over Victorian features, retro aspects, lacey Italian traditional elements, and fake Canadian furs. Marti was breathless with laughter by the end of the evening. "I've had a lovely time. Let's get together again, soon."

Kevin's eyes sparkled: deep, warm, and brown. "Until then, I'll do more research. This is the finest introduction to a new art that I've personally experienced."

"Then we'll make it as good as possible."

The warmth of Kevin's easy acceptance lasted Marti until they met again.

*   *   *

The popularity of Marti's creations blossomed. The more she ventured out in public, the greater the positive responses her Shoebox designs received. She set up a business and began taking orders. Fittings, fabric shopping, and finances filled her days—a welcome change from the old days. Kevin's bright flow of ideas kept her imagination sparking. She gave away freebie miniature samples, designed a plethora of business cards, and at local craft fairs she provided models of her designs for people to try on. Although some customers seemed confused, most loved her Shoeboxes.

As her first profits rolled in, she reveled in the new independence her former problem now brought her. Best of all, instead of dreading being out in the world, not only did she enjoy her outings, but she had the pleasure of seeing how her designs could help others as well—people who shared the same fears she'd had.

I've found my place in the world. This shoebox really fits.

But could she enter the world without it? The question lingered.

* * *

As Marti's business boomed and her friendship with Kevin grew, Carl grew ticked off at her rapidly diminishing spare time and how little of it she was spending with him. "It's a business," Marti kept explaining. "I got the ball rolling, now I have to keep up with it."

Their month was up. They talked about separating. Carl put the final nail in the coffin when he said, "You're spending too much time on fashion and not enough on more important things."

At those words, Marti abruptly changed her mind about her reluctance to lose him. "Important things like what? Cheese?" Kevin would never be that insensitive. "You were the one wanting me to get out more, Carl. Well, I've gotten out. Here I am. I've loved being with you, but I finally got my life going, and I'm not stopping now."

"What do you expect me to do while you're busy with all this?"

"Ride your cycle? How about learning to sew?" She offered him a pile of glossy silver fabric (just flown in from Paris) and a tangle of framing wire.

He rolled his eyes at her.

"Right," she said.

Three days later, Carl moved out. Marti stood at her lonely front door, watching him load the last of his belongings into his pickup truck, her heart filled with mixed emotions.

"Goodbye, Babe." That rugged face of Carl's that Marti had loved revealed a mixture of sadness, confusion, resignation, and the slightest bit of relief. (Marti didn't miss that.) "Keep up the good work. It's been interesting."

Before she could reply, the pickup door slammed and Carl drove away, leaving an empty spot in the driveway. Marti's eyes followed him down the road, past the mailbox where she'd found freedom.

I can do this. She steadied herself. Forget Carl. It was time to try navigating the world without her Shoeboxes.

*   *   *

Marti found that Kevin more than made up for Carl's absence. In fact, Kevin applauded quitting her online job to pour all her time into her fledgling enterprise. Within two months, she had seven employees and glowed with success.

Four months later, with Ava's help, Marti bought a building site and established her own assembly line. Soon, her business roared, producing new designs every week. In a moment of nostalgia, after watching Carl ride by on his motorcycle, she introduced a "wheels" version of her Shoebox. It became her biggest hit of the year.

Orders streamed in from all corners of the globe. The Shoebox Sensation was out, and everyone wanted it. "I guess the shoebox fit after all," she chortled to Kevin, watching her employees scurry around her shop. "To think all this started from a stupid argument."

"A lucky argument for me." Kevin gently touched the lace of her vintage Italian Turn-of-the-Nineteenth-Century Shoebox. "I'd have a stupid argument with you any day and happily lose, just so I can spend more time with you. I love your fascinating solutions to world interaction. You've opened a lot of new doors for me since I met you."

"Oh, you...." Marti rested her head against his shoulder. She loved how Kevin saw only *her*, whether she was wearing a shoebox or not. But would things stay that way? Sooner or later, she'd have to find out.

She chose sooner.

*   *   *

On the one-year anniversary of her Shoebox creations, Marti invited Kevin over and asked, "Would you consider being my assistant production designer?"

"I'd be honored." He gave a deep bow, delicately kissed her hand, then swept her off her feet in a careful hug, spinning her in a circle and making her laugh. "As long as I can keep one foot in the library."

Marti beamed. "It's a deal. We'll split the profits. I've started working on my university and vocational training models."

But Kevin went on, "I have one request."

Marti's heart skipped a beat, her stomach folding in on itself. *Here it comes. I know what he's going to ask.* "Hold on, before you say anything. I'm making a proposal."

He blinked. "Okay."

"Well, maybe I'll just do it." Marti glanced out the picture window of her shop, where the world awaited everyone equally. It was now or never.

Marti quickly pulled off her tangerine spandex work Shoebox (she always wore regular clothes underneath), took a deep breath, and headed for the front door. Her hands went cold and started to sweat. The old panic crept back, sending chills down her spine.

The shop went still. All of her employees watched her, respectfully quiet.

Kevin moved forward but Marti waved him back. "Sorry, I need to do this alone." Remembering how terrifying stepping outside had once been, she hoped that life was still forever behind her.

Only one way to find out. It's not going to get any easier the longer you stand here.

Sweat trickled down Marti's back. With determination fueled by past success, she pushed open the door of her shop—*her own shop*—and stepped outside into the vivid autumn day, for the first time without a Shoebox.

54

The world was just as expansive, the sky just as immense—bright and beautiful and oh so big—as on her first Shoebox expedition to WallShop. The streets were as loud, the people as many. Somehow, although she felt oddly visible, the old panic no longer seized her.

At the sound of applause, she discovered her employees standing at the window, clapping, cheering, and waving at her. Sara, the newest hire, held up a book: *How to Conquer Social Anxiety in Five Steps.* "One massive step!" Sara mouthed, pointing to her. "Write your own book!"

Her face heating in proud embarrassment, Marti gave a deep bow. After a short walk and ten minutes of panicless solitude, she waved Kevin to come join her. "That was the acid test, if that's what you were going to ask me about."

"Actually, it wasn't, but I'm delighted for you." Kevin's brown eyes sparkled with joy. "I was just going to ask you to dinner."

Marti doubled over with laughter. "You're on. Let's go uptown to celebrate. I have some old haunting grounds that'll be great for Shoebox ideas."

"I'm glad you're okay with however you want to be. Really." Kevin took her face gently in his hands. "I love you just as much, with or without your Shoeboxes."

Her eyes filled. "I believe you." She could so easily spend the rest of her life with him. Shoeboxes or not.

At the second anniversary of Marti's Shoebox Designs, profits were soaring. After meticulous searching, Marti bought a new house (one without any sad memories) set on a hillside above town, surrounded by decks and a swimming pool that accommodated up to twenty guests all wearing her "Down to the Coast" Shoebox designs. The house had plenty of workshop space for creativity, as well as nooks and a vaulted room for Kevin's book collections. A gorgeous view included Kevin's beloved library, from which he blew her kisses every morning on the side lawn.

He proposed to her on a beautiful spring day, when the blooming lavender matched her newly released "French Riviera" Shoebox.

They married three months later.

Marti started a new tradition of surprising Kevin each day by choosing whether or not to wear a Shoebox, and every evening they celebrated personal freedom, toasting each other with fine wine and watching the sunset, as her Shoebox sensation swept the world.

Midnight in the Witch's Kitchen

Midnight in the Witch's Kitchen is a harrowing time of magic and mayhem. Some can't cook, while others obtain unexpected results from traditional spells. There's always something brewing in the cauldrons. Grab the ladle and have a taste. Mind the finger food.

https://www.hiraethsffh.com/product-page/midnight-in-the-witch-s-kitchen

I, Gnome: Rise of a Wizard
M. R. Williamson

Not long after the birth of Yenwolk Stonesmith, came the Wizard Basil Alvis to the Stonesmith home. Now, the entire town of Cutoff knew the babe was something more than just a Gnome. As Yen grew, word traveled throughout the countryside that the wizard had sent a 'Watcher' to protect the lad. Coupled with that, and the sighting of an elusive dragon near the Stonesmith home, left no doubt that normality had indeed left the village of Cutoff.

https://www.hiraethsffh.com/product-page/i-gnome-rise-of-a-wizard-by-m-r-williamson

trailblazers and visionaries
Lee Clark Zumpe

this is where we begin:
trailblazers and visionaries establishing a foothold –
pressurized habitats, domed agricultural zones,
sprawling subsurface communities.

this is where we transform:
landscape architects and topography engineers,
climate modification by technological manipulation,
remapping a barren, frozen landscape.

this is where we breathe:
meticulous, far-reaching alteration and adaption –
generating an artificial magnetosphere
preventing solar winds from stripping the new
atmosphere.

this is where we thrive:
self-expansion and self-sustenance –
forging a complex biosphere
populated with genetically modified organisms.

this is where we survive:
establishing off-world settlements,
flourishing communities crowded with expatriates –
colonization overrides extinction by ecological collapse.

The Caged Bird and the Fairy
Matias Travieso-Diaz

*The caged bird sings with a fearful trill
of things unknown but longed for still
for the caged bird sings of freedom.*
Maya Angelou

Roger fluttered excitedly as he sought to approach the strange bird that was hovering outside Roger's bamboo cage. The cage was large and Roger small (a mere five inches from crest to tail) so he had plenty of space to roam back and forth, in and out, but he could never get close enough to his target. The bird outside the cage was also small, but the similarities ended there. Roger was a male Pacific parrotlet, a small parrot with a dusty grey cast over the body, a bright green mask, and a pinkish beak; the stranger was translucent, with diaphanous wings whose colors changed constantly and a body that mimicked that of Adrianne, the youngest of his human owners.

"Who are you?" Roger intended to say, but what came out of his beak was a loud "tchit" that he repeated, over and again. The other bird remained silent, and Roger resorted to other sounds in his repertory, imitating the noises humans made and those from Edith, the family's striped white and gray cat. There was no reply to any of them.

Roger was starting to lose interest in the other bird when a series of images formed in his brain: a sun-drenched meadow adorned with all sorts of flowers; fields of low bushes from which grew stalks of grain, an expanse of turquoise water at whose edge wavelets broke into a golden beach dotted with tall, bending trees that could have come from Roger's ancestral home; limitless blue skies dotted with fluffy white clouds; mountains, prairies, placid rivers, all of which beckoned him.

"Wouldn't you want to be here?" was the images' silent entreaty.

These feelings were new and confusing. Roger had been hatched in captivity and had progressed from confinement in a pet shop to a similar situation at the home of his current owners. Roger was abundantly fed quinoa, millet, broccoli, beetroot, oats, bell peppers, rice, and pomegranate seeds, although his favorites were fruits of all kinds. He was given exercise periods outside his cage, and often sat himself on the shoulder of one of his owners. He lived alone, having pecked to death his consort Brigitte in a fit of temper several years back, but managed to entertain himself by imitating the noises humans made and the growls of Edith. He felt content living in his bamboo home, in the living room of his owners. What need did he have to go to those alien places?

Roger was able to locate the source of these visions: they seemed to originate from the strange bird, which was still circling around his cage annoyingly. Roger uttered a quick series of unwelcoming "tchits" and bumped repeatedly against the walls of the cage to evidence his displeasure. The strange bird, however, remained unfazed. "Let's go see places with me," it seemed to suggest.

The suggestion did not resonate with Roger. Though he descended from many generations of long-distance travelers accustomed to traverse mile upon mile of the Amazon jungle, he was only used to short flights within and around his cage and did not feel adventurous. He issued a couple of energetic "tchits" in negation and planted himself on his perch, determined to ignore the obnoxious visitor.

But the visitor was not about to give up so easily. It flew right up to the cage, gyrated twice, and issued from one of its extremities a shaft of bright light that burned a hole on the gate that sealed the cage. There was a smell of burned wood and the gate became unlocked, its remains hanging uselessly from its hinges. The bird made an unmistakable "Follow me!" motion with its humanlike hands and darted out towards an open window. After a while, curiosity won over and Roger gave chase.

****

They flew wildly, rising and falling and twirling in the air currents, chasing each other, and letting the sun warm their wings, in endless enjoyment of the glorious summer afternoon. Roger decided that, after all, he liked the adventure. But the good feelings were not meant to last; soon the dark figure of a falcon appeared in the sky and gave chase, seeking to capture one or both frolickers. It got to Roger first, and held the parrot's tail firmly in its talons intending to bring its victim within reach of its sharp beak, but before it could complete its attack it was struck by an energy bolt discharged by the other bird, which hovered in mid air above the pair and signaled Roger to fly away.

Roger reacted by plummeting in the general direction of the home of its owners, which he was instinctively able to locate as he slowed his descent a few meters above the ground. He entered through the same open window that had allowed him to depart only a short time earlier, and flew into the remains of his cage, where he perched himself shivering while he stared fearfully for a potential pursuit by the falcon.

The falcon was otherwise occupied. It had lunged at the strange bird and torn off one of its wings, sending the bird spiraling down to earth, out of control. The falcon gave chase, but another blast of energy from its prey caused the predator to seek safety by flying away precipitously. The falling bird somehow managed to slow down its descent and entered the house through the same window that Roger had used for his escape. It coasted down to the floor and lay there, not moving.

All the commotion did not go unnoticed. Edith woke up from her afternoon nap and moseyed on into the living room. She came to a halt when she detected a bird lying on the floor and moved up to the strange creature, smelling its body and trying to figure out if it was edible. Soon she decided that, if not to eat, the object was at least good to play with and picked the bird off the floor with her mouth and started pawing its body trying to clicit a reaction from it.

Edith did get her reaction, but it came from an unexpected source. Roger darted across the room and began pecking viciously at the cat's ears. Edith was surprised: she was familiar with this bird, who sat day and night in an out of reach cage and annoyingly imitated Edith's grunts and meows, and was treated by the humans as a household member. Roger's pecking was drawing blood from Edith's ears and was intolerable, so the cat dropped the strange bird and turned towards Roger, trying to swat at him with her paws. Roger, however, was too fast and kept moving randomly, remaining out of reach.

Meanwhile, the strange bird had recovered and gathered enough strength to fling another blast of energy at the cat's tail, singeing it and causing Edith to yell in pain. Under attack from two directions, Edith thought the better of it and ran back to the safety of the kitchen.

Roger flew down to the floor and inspected the strange bird. It seemed to be recovering; in fact, it was starting to grow a new wing to replace the one it had lost to the falcon. An image of the two birds flying together formed in Roger's mind. It was accompanied by a pleasant feeling and an invitation that suggested that both birds should continue to keep each other's company, and enjoy venturing into the wild together.

Roger did not have the words to express its agreement, but bumped his head gently against the strange bird and issued a low "tchit" to confirm his satisfaction.

And they became good friends and had many adventures together; no cats or birds of prey ever figured in them.

On Holy Ground
Mitchell D. Kowitz

The Minnesota Art Fair is the place to be in the summertime and this year was no exception. It was raining on the opening day of the Art Fair. I fancy myself as an amateur collector of art and was excited to see what treasures I may come across at this year's art fair. I look forward to this event every year and it has now become an annual tradition for me...a little rain certainly wasn't going to dampen my spirits and keep me away.

As in past years, this year's art fair had the usual line up of artists and displays. There were booths of watercolors, ceramics, pottery, and many other original works of art. During my outing, I passed by a booth called House of Redgate. There was a woman named Denise with reddish burgundy colored hair that was piled up on her head in a sort of messy, curly bun. Denise was dressed in a colorful funky type of blouse and jeans accompanied by artsy earrings and other jewelry. Her make-up possessed a certain dramatic flair. Denise had large expressive brown eyes and there was a special aura about her. When she smiled it was very inviting and almost magical. She welcomed me inside her booth and began to show me various pieces of art from her collection. The colors she used in her art were striking and vivid. She worked in several mediums of art and specialized in gothic art and which included vampires and coffins. I remember as a kid going to a lot of horror movies on Saturday afternoons. During the week, there was always some sort of Dracula movie on the theater's bill. Since I loved this type of art, several pieces of Denise's art caught my eye, and I ended up purchasing a few pieces from her. I lingered in her booth and talked with Denise a bit longer...For some odd reason, even though I had just met this woman, I didn't want our conversation to end. I found myself becoming completely captivated by her and her art. Eventually, we said our goodbyes. After visiting a few more booths, I headed back to my car and drove home.

Once I arrived home, I went to work to find special places where I could display my new art. As I was placing one of the coffins, I happened to notice that one of the hinges on it was broken. Fortunately, while in Denise's booth, I grabbed one of her business cards, so I gave her a call. I must admit, I was happy that I had another reason to connect with her. Denise answered the phone, and I could tell by the sound of her voice that she was happy to have another opportunity to talk with me as well. She said that I could stop by her studio anytime and she would repair it for me. Her studio was in her house in Northeast Minneapolis.

The next day I took the drive to Northeast Minneapolis and arrived at 1926 Mockingbird Lane. It was an old two-story Victorian house with red paint on the side and flowers and shrubs near the entrance. There was a big sign in red and gold in the front yard that read "House of Redgate."

I thought to myself... well... this place looks like it is going to be interesting.

Denise was there to meet me at the front door. I walked into the small front of the house, and it was like entering Geppetto's workshop. On either wall were dolls of all shapes and sizes. There were ceramic bulldogs waiting to be painted, and on clay turtles' jewelry was placed around the feet and neck of each one of them. A real work in progress if you ask me.

Denise invited me into the main room. Once I stepped in there, I couldn't believe my eyes...there was so much to take in...it was the most fascinating space I had ever been in. There were several displays and curio cabinets that housed many unique collections from various periods of time in history. My favorite of them all was the Egyptian Queen Sarcophagus. There must have been thousands of items in her collection. For some reason, something came over me and I was drawn to the sarcophagus and felt compelled to touch it.

Once my hands touched the sarcophagus, I began feeling lightheaded and as though I was about to lose my balance. The entire room was spinning round and my mind completely blanked out. I felt my eyes roll into the back of my head and my body began to shake violently.

Suddenly, I found myself transported back in time to an Egyptian court with musicians and performers putting on a show for the Pharoah. On either side of the room were huge fires burning. There were large banquet tables filled with a wide assortment of exotic fruits and meats. In one direction women adorned with colorful scarves, miniature cymbals on their fingers and bells on their feet were gyrating and dancing while keeping perfect tempo with the Middle Eastern style of music. In one corner of the room, there were magicians performing various tricks. There was smoke coming from the abundant fragrant incense that was permeating the air. Snakes were also slithering on the ground.

I finally released my hands from the sarcophagus and immediately fell to the floor. I had difficulty catching my breath and sweat was pouring down my forehead. My hands felt as though electricity had just gone through them.

Denise rushed over to me and asked if I was okay.

I said, "I have just been to ancient Egypt!"

Once I regained my composure, the two of us sat down in the dining room for a cup of coffee. Denise explained that when she bought the house several years ago, the neighbors told her that the house was haunted. She said that she believed that without a doubt, the house had a strange and powerful energy. She went on to tell me that most of the land around here had been used as an ancient Indian burial site. No one knows exactly where these sites are and how many of them exist.

I said to her, "I really don't feel so well…"

At that point, Denise had me lie down on the couch for a while…she then shared with me that this was not the first time that something like this has happened. Many people who have come into her studio and home and picked up a piece of art, say they have experienced a sort of out of body sensation.

"I have often wondered about this house and its origins," she said. "I believe that this house possesses a special energy and mysterious properties."

As I got ready to leave, she informed me that the sarcophagus was one of her favorites and was not for sale. On the way home, I couldn't stop thinking about what happened at Denise's studio. I thought perhaps I was just dehydrated and needed to drink more water.

Then I realized that what happened to me was not a result of me just being dehydrated...something out of this world took place in that house. I know what I felt and when I touched that statue, my hands were filled with electricity. Something's going on in that house that I just cannot explain...but I vowed to find out!

Days went by and I just couldn't stop thinking about the "House of Redgate" and Denise. None of the small gothic art pieces that I bought did anything when I touched them. It was not at all like the sarcophagus.

"It has to be that house" I thought to myself. "There is some kind of energy there."

Time went by and each day, I found myself thinking more and more about Denise. I really wanted to call her but couldn't think of a good excuse that would be believable. As luck would have it, I ended up getting a promotion at my job resulting in my move into a new larger, corner office. There was room for a large art piece on the left corner side of the office. This was the excuse that I needed to give Denise another call. I quickly went to the phone and dialed her number. When she finally answered the phone, I felt my heart begin to beat faster. Truth be told, this was more than just wanting to buy additional pieces of art. I found myself very attracted to Denise, and I felt a strong chemistry between us. I definitely wanted to see her again. She said that she would be in her studio tomorrow afternoon and that I could drop by anytime. I was excited to be able to see her again and I arrived promptly at the House of Redgate around 3:30 p.m.

When I arrived, Denise welcomed me in and asked, "What exactly are you looking for?" I responded, "I really don't know." I began to walk around looking at statues of animals, trolls, witches, gargoyles, clocks, there was such an odd assortment of so many different creations.

She then asked me, "How much room do you have for the piece?"

I showed her the area with my hands, and she said that I could do one piece or a display.

As I walked around her studio one thing caught my eye. It was a huge, hand carved and detailed Grandfather clock. It was majestic in its size and stature and had a wood inlay on the top that went out into a canopy over a horse and carriage. The sides had detailed carvings of angel faces and near the bottom were vines and a tree in the center of the base.

I walked over and slowly put my hands on the clock.

Once again...A strange feeling began to come over me. I felt dizzy and lightheaded. I began to sweat and felt my eyes rolling back into my head. I started to hear people talking and the crackle of a roaring fire in the background.

Suddenly, I was thrust back to a house at the turn of the century. There was the smell of fresh baked bread in the kitchen. I could see in my mind horse carriages through two big stained-glass windows as I looked outside. The house had a large fireplace, two couches and three chairs. Each chair had a small reading table and glasses for whiskey beside it. I started to scream out.

Then...in an instant...Denise grabbed my hands and released them from the clock.

"What did you see?" she asked.

"Where am I?" I asked.

"You are in my home...the House of Redgate.

You just put your hands on the grandfather clock and began to go into some type of trance."

"I need to sit down for a while." I said.

I sat down on the couch and Denise said, "You know...not everybody sees things, but I have been told by people that do."

So...once again... Denise asked, "What did you see?"

I began to tell her about the house and fireplace and the horses that I saw outside.

"That's simply a gift." she said.

"How is this possible?" I asked.

She said, "Energy.

I believe there is an energy curve in this house that can somehow distort time."

"I don't know about that" I replied, "but I do know what I felt and what I saw!"

We arranged a day and time for me to send movers out to her home to pick up the grandfather clock. After an awkward silence, I finally got up the nerve to ask Denise out for a date. I let her know that I really enjoy her company and that I would like to see her other than just buying art from her.

Denise looked a bit taken back then smiled at me and said, "I would love to." We made plans for that Friday evening to go out for dinner and a movie.

The clock was delivered on Tuesday, and I had it placed in a side corner in my office. The clock looked so majestic standing proudly in the corner. Several people walked by my office and commented on the clock's amazing wood carvings...especially the angels, the tree, and the vines.

Again, I started to think about what had happened in Denise's home. I walked slowly over to the clock. Took a deep breath and put my hands on it expecting to go back to that old turn of the century house.

Nothing... Nothing at all.

I stood there with my hands on that clock for about five more minutes. Still nothing. I thought... this is so odd.

I had a lot of work to do, so the rest of the day became refocused on work...totally consumed with paperwork.

While working, I thought about what Denise had said about the energy in the house. Perhaps it was true. She did say that all on the property and all around it were supposedly sacred Indian burial grounds. Perhaps this holds the key to the power in that house.

A friend of mine, Peter Jones, a tall drink of water type of man who was around six foot, five inches tall, was a psychologist at City University. He also had a huge hobby of exploring paranormal phenomena. I called him and during our conversation, told him all about the House of Redgate and the experiences I had there. I asked him if he would consider exploring this house in more depth with me, permitting of course that Denise would be agreeable to this.

Peter said that he didn't have to think about it... he was in!

After I hung up with Peter, I called Denise and explained to her about my friend Peter and that his hobby was paranormal phenomena. I then asked her if it would be alright for us to set up a time to come over to do a sort of paranormal investigation to check the house for paranormal energy and activity. Denise agreed and we set up a time to come over the following day.

Once we arrived at the House of Redgate, Denise welcomed Peter and I in. Denise took us to the main room and made us some herbal tea with honey and lemon and brought us some of her freshly baked scones. Over the tea and scones, I asked Denise, "Do you know how old the house is?"

Denise said that she had no idea but knew for sure that the house was at least 100 years old.

Before our meeting on Wednesday, I had gone downtown to the courthouse to look up the history of the house and the property it sat on. My research revealed that dating back to the early 1600s, several square miles of the land had belonged to the La Cota Indian tribe. I wondered to myself if the house could in fact be on or near holy ground. That is a terminology often used to denote a religious or burial site. No information pointed me in that direction but nonetheless, it had to be a possibility I thought.

Peter had brought some equipment with him that was able to measure sound waves and distortions as well as thermal energy. We set this equipment up in specific areas of each room.

I asked Peter to touch a Statue of David..." nothing" he said. Peter started to take readings and once again,

Denise said to me, "Sometimes people feel something and sometimes they don't."

"There are definite wave patterns that I am detecting." Peter said. "Some are quite different than others."

Peter then took some of the equipment with him and walked out into the yard. I heard him yell out, "Very strong readings out here and several places have spiked the machine."

"The Indian tribe of the Lakota is said to have many unmarked burial sites in Minnesota" Denise said. Perhaps this could be one. Denise went on further and said, "There were many shamans or "Holy Men" in the Lakota tribe. Could it be that this house is sitting on energy from shamans who have passed away?"

Peter came back into the house and noted that there were energy discrepancies and said that we now know this from the readings.

Could this be from past entities that once lived on this land? All of these thoughts were now coming to a head. We now have the ability to measure energy in ways that we never had before.

I watched Denise as she just stood there silently in a corner. She began to tell us that for many years, she has had unexplained dreams of Indian dances and ritual practices. "Over many years and nights, I have dreamed of watching the elders from the tribes' dance and sing their songs. I feel like I have lived with these people before." she said.

"It's clear that there is something here... but time mental transportation?"

said a very skeptical Peter.

I then looked at Denise with wide eyes and asked, "Do you see visions when you hold and touch objects in this house?"

She hesitated and then said, "Yes...I do."

She went on, "As I said, some people feel things, and some do not. The people that don't feel...don't believe. The people who do feel...believe."

Denise went on..." Maybe this energy is a conduit for what we might call faith...if it is strong inside of you, it opens up a place of possibilities."

Peter exclaimed, "I really don't know about any of that stuff."

But I did...and I knew that I wasn't going crazy.

Something happens to objects in and around this house and property. As in Indian culture, the power of spirts live on to fulfill another destiny.

Before we left, Denise looked at Peter and I in a deep and most serious way. "You must never tell anyone about this...if you do, my life and this house will never be the same."

Peter and I just looked at each other and knew that Denise was right. We had to keep Denise's secret and as hard as it was, we had to take this secret to our graves. I thought to myself, perhaps this is why objects already in this house are affected with this energy portal syndrome. In any case, we both promised to keep the secret of this house. We got into the car and didn't say a word all the way back home.

The next day, I woke up and arrived at work at 7:30 a.m. I made coffee for my coworkers and went inside my office. There on the left corner of my office, stood that majestic grandfather clock.

It beckoned me to come closer. I approached the clock slowly, raised both of my hands and put each one on either side against the clock. I closed my eyes and just stood there waiting for a sign.

Hoping for another gift of a vision, but to my disappointment...nothing...it was just as it was before.

We all use our five senses to make our way in this world. But the sixth sense can be called our sense of faith. And faith, in its essence, is energy.

Friday arrived, and Denise and I finally went out on our first official date. It was a chilly, windswept rainy evening. We ended up tucking into a cute little trendy restaurant in Denise's neighborhood called The Wharf. We both ordered the fish and chips. Over dinner, we talked and talked, it was as though we had known each other for many years or perhaps in another lifetime. Once we finished our dinner, we walked a block up the street to a little independent theater where they had a midnight double feature. They were showing Rosemary's Baby and Children of a Lesser God. During the first intermission, several people around us got out of their seats and headed to the lobby. Since Denise and I were practically alone in the dark theater, I reached over and surprised her with a kiss that nearly took her breath away. Denise was so receptive to my affection that she kissed me back and I nearly lost my breath as well. The rest of the movie Denise and I sat extra close to each other, and I had my arm around her.

After the movie was over, we headed back to the car where we held each other and kissed several times. Both of us professed how our feelings had grown and deepened for each other.

More than a year has passed since that windswept rainy night. Denise and I have remained together. I too, now live in Redgate Manor with Denise and all her unique collections. With each passing day, our love continues to deepen and grow, and we are very happy together. Not in my wildest dreams would I have ever thought I would be in love with such a woman and living in such a house!

From time to time, I think back on the paranormal events that took place and ultimately brought us together as a couple. I have come to realize that house and property were entrusted to Denise and now also to me to guard and protect. I guess you could say that overall, Denise and I are caretakers of sorts...she has known all along what I finally came to realize...

That we live on Holy Ground.

In Days to Come

By Lisa Timpf

The poems in this collection are grouped into four sections. The first, "Terra, Terra," includes poems set on the planet Earth. That is true of many of the poems in the second section, "Looming Shadows," though they have been grouped together in relation to some of the potential disasters we as a human race have set ourselves up for—nuclear warfare, climate change, and so on. "Alien Encounters" contains poems relating to imagined interactions with other space-faring species. "Other Worlds" rounds out the collection with speculations on what life might be like if and when humanity spins out to the stars.

Print Edition: https://www.hiraethsffh.com/product-page/in-days-to-come-by-lisa-timpf

ePub: https://www.hiraethsffh.com/product-page/in-days-to-come-by-lisa-timpf-2

Tales From the Quantum Café
by Alan Ira Gordon

A collection of oddments created over lunch—you'll find them in this volume. There's an homage to the Thimble Theater; a treatment of the Revolutionary War in terms of a baseball game; small-town environmental problems; a random pun here and there; life on the Outback; the secret of the Drake equation; an off-beat look at Disney; and much, much more!

https://www.hiraethsffh.com/product-page/tales-from-the-quantum-cafe-by-alan-ira-gordon